The Background Music

A story about Love, Friendship and Memories which refuse to fade away.

"Dedicated to my sister Dhriti, for asking me the same question Vikas asked Akansha in Chapter 12. Read along to find out."

You remember your first love because they show you, prove to you, that you can love and be loved . That, nothing is deserved except love and love is both how you become a person and why.

By John Green (Turtles All The Way Down)

ABOUT THE AUTHOR

Born on 23.11.2011 in Jalandhar Punjab. He started his relationship with pen and paper at the age of 9.

He completed his first novel at the age of 13.

He believes that age is not a barrier while accomplishing your dreams.

What you are holding in your hand is the debut novel of the author.

Please submit your reviews at:-

- Amazon

- Flipkart

- Notionpress.com

- tathyatheyoungwriter@gmail.com

About the Book

On an ordinary day, in an ordinary college, Akansha Trivedi receives 3 messages from VIkas, a boy she had not talked to for 6 long years. And the messages don't make any sense.

"Akansha, I do not know whom to trust anymore. But I had to tell somebody, so I thought about you."

"I am going to Finland. I need to escape."

"Do not message me back, as I am going to break my phone and shatter it into pieces so that no one can track me. I do not know why I thought about you. Have a great life."

Akansha, along with her best friend, Vaishnavi, embark on a crazy journey to find Vikas and solve the mystery of the messages.

A Story about Love, Friendship and Memories that refuse to fade away, The Background Music, won't let you leave till the last page.

<u>1</u>

Friends are like F.M. They don't help us reach the destination but make the journey more fun. Hi, I am Akansha Trivedi. I teach at the Rani Lakshmi Bai College in Ahmedabad. I live in a rented apartment with my friend Vaishnavi. Crazy things happen so often in my life that it is a shame to even call them crazy. I mean, crazy things are a part of my routine—not something you would expect from a 25-year-old professor.

The major thing is that it is not like one crazy event triggered all the craziness. Even though meeting Vaishnavi has contributed significantly to many things. Okay, if this book were from her point of view, she would probably say that meeting me was a major contribution to the craziness in her life because, well, we are both sort of crazy. And if we have someone with whom we can be crazy, and that person is also sort of crazy, and she also has someone with whom she can be crazy—believe me, the 'sort of crazy' would become so crazy that—okay, never mind. I do not want to scare you from day one.

Anyway, what I was saying is that all the crazy things are not linked to each other. Like: Crazy

Thing x is not equal to crazy thing y. LHS is not equal to RHS. Hence proved that I am a Maths teacher because who on Earth uses Maths to express her feelings?

<u>2</u>

I was explaining trigonometry to a bunch of second-year students when my mobile beeped. I did not want to check my phone in the middle of an important lecture. My phone beeped again, and I had to put it on silent to stop myself from being distracted. Anyway, it was probably just Vaishnavi. Unlike me, she did not have classes to take. She is a freelancer and earns by writing stories and poems for different magazines and newspapers.

We met in Kota, a place where students go to convert themselves into machines. I was forced to go there and study to get into IIT. Well, I was not exactly forced to become an IITian. I was also given the choice of becoming a doctor and preparing for the NEET exam-the two classic choices my Indian parents gave me. I did not want to seal my fate by becoming a doctor, so I decided to become an engineer. Because if you study medicine, you have to become a doctor, but if you are an engineer, you could be so many things: a writer, an artist, an IAS officer, a cop, a businessperson, an Ola driver, or in this case, a professor.

Vaishnavi was also in Kota, also forced by her parents to become a doctor. Both of us never cleared the exams, as you can see. After that, we left Kota and came to Delhi. I had been admitted to the prestigious St. Stephen's College in Delhi, and Vaishnavi decided to come along in search of jobs. She got a job at a private school as an English teacher. She also began writing stories, and we had some more notes in our house. Since then, she has been working on a novel, which has been turned down by publishers. When I graduated and got a job at the Rani Lakshmi Bai College, where I am teaching now, she left her job as she was earning more money by writing stories than by explaining them to some 12-year-olds anyway.

The lecture ended, and I went into the corridor to check my phone. I had three messages from Vikas.

"Akansha, I do not know whom to trust anymore. But I had to tell somebody, so I thought about you."

"I am going to Finland. I need to escape."

"Do not message me back, as I am going to break my phone and shatter it into pieces so that no one can track me. I do not know why I thought about you. Have a great life."

With these messages, Vikas Gupta either threw his phone hard or hit it with a hammer or something like that, leaving me confused. I read and reread those messages again and again. With each time I reached the end words, my confusion just grew and grew and grew. I filed for emergency leave and rushed home. I needed my sort-of-crazy friend.

<u>**3**</u>

Vaishnavi was typing furiously on her second-hand laptop when I reached our apartment.

"What, bhai, you came early," she said without taking her gaze off the screen.

"Vaishnavi," I was not able to say more. Words failed me.

I think she could hear that I was panting. I think she could also hear my heart as it pumped blood. She looked at me and realized that something was amiss.

"What happened?" she asked.

I passed her the phone, and I think, like me, she also reread it several times.

"Akku," she said and hugged me.

The dam inside me broke, and tears filled my eyes.

"Do not worry. I am here," she said. Those three words had the power to drift me away, pulling me back into the past.

<u>4</u>

Six Years Ago...

I walked into my room, exhausted. Vaishnavi was already sitting there, drinking some green liquid. I sat down on the chair. But I was not feeling like resting. After attending eight classes—each more boring than the last—it was enough to make you desperately want to do something. I really wanted to play something hard. People can get really anxious if they do not play sports, especially if they are addicted to them to the extent that they carry bats on picnics.

"What is the green liquid you are drinking?" I asked, tossing a grape into my mouth.

Vaishnavi always had grapes near her. Do not ask me why. She was always found eating something. She had a sort of cow-like personality—always munching on something or the other. I wonder why she is not fat—probably because she munches on grapes, not grape-based drinks.

"Green tea," she replied. "Kota sucks."

And here she began her daily routine of abusing Kota. I wonder how Kota is prosperous despite the curses of students. Well, probably because of the students. I mean, no one cares about my curses. Everybody cares about the money we pay to go to a hellhole.

"Yaar, let's eat something. I am hungry. I don't want to eat grapes," I said, hunger mice jumping in my stomach.

"No point. A cold sandwich costs 100 rupees," she said, cursing the hostel canteen.

"Let's go out then. We can have some street food," I said, desperately hungry now.

I also had a plan. Normally, Vaishnavi would not agree to play cricket, but the mention of food could surely get her out. And if she came along, and I carried the bats and balls, she probably wouldn't be able to reject the offer.

As we walked toward the samosa-kachori wala, I thought about my future for the millionth time. Would IIT actually help me, or was I just wasting my time on a useless degree?

I revisited the carefully woven plan I had stitched together—how I would revolutionize the education system, start a school focused on practical knowledge, and eventually expand it into a full-fledged board like CBSE.

I envisioned nurturing bright young minds, guiding them to create real-world solutions instead of just writing about them in exams. These students wouldn't just learn—they would innovate, building anything they could dream of. It was the only way India could solve problems like pollution and road accidents.

You may wonder, if I want to start a school based on practical learning, IIT may actually prove to be helpful. I mean, literally, its full form is the Indian Institute of Technology. But the thing is that I am not very innovative myself. However, I can still start my school by hiring experts in this field.

I felt bad that I was not able to do anything. An urge to make something happen gripped me harder and harder. I felt heavy—not because of responsibility, but because I could not take action.

I promised myself that I would make this happen. At least, I would try my best.

The wind blew freely, and I felt light again. If wind were a person, I would have gazed at it for a long time.

The best part about the best things in life is that you can't see them alone. You never see the wind, but as you feel its presence, you realize that it makes you feel light.

You see smiles, but you can't see happiness.

You never see the best things alone. Like, you can't see samosas alone—they are always best accompanied by chutneys.

Vaishnavi was typing something on her machine. I could see that she was onto something big, like she did not even once remark about the flavor of kachoris. Even Ramu Bhaiya, our street vendor, looked puzzled and gave me a questioning glance, pointing at her. I shrugged my shoulders—I had as little clue as Ramu Bhaiya did.

She stayed on the phone for a long time, even after we had finished eating.

"Vaish, can't you leave your stupid phone for once? The weather is so nice," I said, a little irritated.

She did not listen to me, or she pretended not to. Irritating girl.

"Vaish!" I increased my volume.

"Huh!" she said as if she had heard the words, but her system was unable to register them.

"I am saying that the weather is nice, and we should play cricket," I said, modifying my voice like the one we use for babies.

"Wait a minute, I am onto something," she said.

"We don't have much time; we have to study a lot, Vaish," I said, trying to convince her.

She took her gaze off her phone and looked at me.

"Tell me honestly, do you want to go to IIT?"

"Not really, but..."

"Then who cares if we study or not?" she said, cutting me mid-sentence.

That is the thing that I like most about Vaishnavi—the clarity she has about life. When the whole Kota is lying awake to study, she lies awake to write stories. I waited for her to complete this project.

After quite some time, she came back with a triumphant smile.

"Look," she said, handing me her phone.

Shahrukh Khan danced on the screen as the music played:

"Kiska hain re tumko intezaar, main hoon na. Dekh lo idhar bhi ek baar, main hoon na."

Translated to:

"Whom are you waiting for? I am here. Just look here once, I am here."

"What on earth is this? A Shahrukh Khan fan club or something?" I said.

"No, bhai, it is not a fan club. It is a psychology app."

The song continued:

"Pa ke khoya hain agar pyaar, main hoon na. Ho raha hain dil bekaraar, main hoon na."

Translated to:

"If you have lost love after getting it, I am here. If you are getting restless, I am here."

"But these are not the real lyrics of the song," I protested.

"Yeah, bhai, it is the app's own lyrics to tell us about its purpose. So, look, whenever we want any help or need to rant our problems to someone, this app is there."

"Pretty cool," I said.

"How much did it cost, by the way?"

"This app is called 'I Am Here.' It cost ₹799 for a year," she said like she was the brand ambassador of I.A.H.

"Can we play cricket now?" I asked.

"Yes, but I will bat," she said, picking up the willow bat.

<u>**5**</u>

Okay, I am not as stressless and carefree as my companion. I mean, I freaked out when I realized that it was 8 PM, and I had not studied a word. I picked up my books and began revising Newton's laws of motion. I thought I was following the subject, but when I began solving numericals, I realized that I sucked at physics.

At 12, I lay in bed, but sleep was far from my eyes. I tossed and turned in bed, unable to sleep. I suddenly got the temptation to look at my phone— I don't know why. And then an argument began in my brain between the rational and emotional parts of my mind.

Rational Brain: You are trying to sleep. Checking your phone won't help.

Emotional Brain: You only have to check the phone once.

R: You won't be able to leave your phone after just taking a glance. And what do you even want to see on your phone? Screens should be avoided at night before sleeping. You should take some deep breaths if you want to sleep.

E: You are not a professional. You should ask in I.A.H. It is the app run by psychologists. They will give better advice.

My rational brain relented. I picked up the phone and reduced the volume to zero—I did not want Vaishnavi to wake up with the heavy noise. I pressed the chat button. Vikas happened to be my consultant.

Me: Hi!

Him: Hi, let me guess. You are unable to sleep because who texts a psychologist in the middle of the night?

Me: Okay, that's not a bad judgment, but first of all, I want to say our app's mechanism is weird. I mean, we pay to type messages and just be ensured that the other person on the line is a good listener. Even if he is listening to earn his bread. I mean, you get paid to listen.

Him: That is not very well summarized. We give professional advice on day-to-day problems, and even if what you said was true, what's weird in that? In every seller-buyer relationship, the buyer pays to get something. In this case, what you get is not exactly material like bread, pen, or whatever, but they are good feelings and clarity. Even when they are non-materialistic does not mean they don't have value.

Me: Tell me why I am unable to sleep?

Him: Your brain has a mechanism. There are three parts of this—a Rational Decision Maker, a Monkey, and a Panic Monster.

So basically, what happens is that when we have to do any task, let's say, complete an assignment, our rational decision maker tells us to do it on time, but our Monkey keeps procrastinating. But when the night before submission comes, the Panic Monster gets activated. The Monkey is super afraid of the Panic Monster, so it runs away, and then we start to work.

But this mechanism proves to be useless in this case because we are trying to sleep, and we need to be relaxed to sleep. But when the Panic Monster comes, your state of mind is anything but relaxed, and because of that, you are unable to sleep. This causes more panic, and it becomes more difficult to sleep, and the cycle continues.

I was charmed by this Vikas. He had logic.

"So, what should I do?" I typed back.

Him: You need to relax yourself, and you can take some deep breaths to relax your brain.

Me: Okay, thanks.

My rational brain was right after all.

Him: You are welcome, Vaishnavi.

Me: I am not Vaishnavi. I am her friend, Akansha. I have used her ID and password so I don't have to pay double.

I don't know why I confessed. Maybe I trusted Vikas.

Understandable. He replied with a grinning emoji.

<u>6</u>

Once, a study was conducted by some scientists. People were shown pictures of random faces and asked to rate them on various factors such as attractiveness and trustworthiness. It was observed that the ratings fluctuated when viewers stared at a picture for longer than a specific period—*but only for attractiveness*. The ratings for trustworthiness remained constant. This is because humans evolved to make snap judgments about trustworthiness when we lived as hunter-gatherers.

The point is that my immediate impression of Vikas was that he could be trusted. I had dozed off after a few breaths, perhaps it was because his advice was genuine, or maybe I simply felt a natural trust in him that had comforted me to sleep.`

I found myself texting Vikas quite often. He told me that I was lonely. He also mentioned that he was in 12th grade and working in I.A.H to earn some money for college.

I couldn't tell if he shared his personal life with everyone, even though our conversation was supposed to be about me. Somehow, that made me feel special. but, why would I be special? I was just another customer to him .

Time slipped by as it is supposed to be, and before I knew it, I found myself wandering the empty streets of Kota. I passed by hostel rows where no one was around, and I missed the children who used to play cricket in the parks. I missed the warmth of Amritsar—where people lived life fully rather than like machines.

It was evening, a beautiful time when birds return to their nests. I, too, wanted to go back. I longed to fly toward my mission, that longing gripped me so fiercely it sometimes felt suffocating. I wanted to tell Vikas that I wasn't lonely—I was merely far away from my dream. So I pulled out my phone and just did that.

Almost immediately, he replied:

"Hum— as a psychologist, I would say that you should find something here that matches your passion. For example, if you want to be a teacher, start by taking your friends' doubts. But as a friend, I would tell you to walk away if you don't want it."

I stared at his message for a long time, grateful for two reasons:

1. He had said exactly what I needed to hear.
2. He had used the word "friend."

Friends are like F.M. But sometimes, they can also become Google Maps . I still remember that day as if it were yesterday. It was April 10, 2019—my **JEE exam** was scheduled for the 20th of the month. Vaishnavi's NEET was on May 5, and sleep had practically been eliminated from the Kota curriculum. This was the day after my conversation with Vikas, and I shared our plan to escape from this place with Vaishnavi. She was very excited about the prospect.

We had just Rs. 5000 in her pocket—mostly earned through her writing and a little sent by my parents. Our plan was simple:

- I and Vaishnavi would go to Delhi.

- **I** wanted to study economics and math for my business, so I would try to get into Saints Stephen College, a prestigious institution.
- Vaishnavi would also seek employment as a teacher and, after school, continue writing stories.
- We would rent an apartment. Besides, I believed that Vaishnavi would also get the

money and support she needed from her parents, even if she was initially sceptical. Her parents would have to accept her dream of becoming a writer.

With this plan in mind, we stood at the bus stand waiting for the bus that would take us to our dreams. When it finally arrived, we climbed aboard.

The journey to our dreams was bumpy—full of literal and metaphorical potholes. It all added to the craziness of the situation. Vaishnavi had even bought a novel titled *Delhi Is Not Far* by Ruskin Bond. As she turned through the pages, I rested my head on her shoulder and gazed out the window, where I saw three boys playing cricket. I smiled— my dreams were, in a small way, coming true.

The best part about crazy things is how comfortably you can sleep when they're happening.Throughout the bus ride to Delhi, I had my head resting on Vaishnavi's shoulder. Soon enough, Vaishnavi woke me up.

"Bhai, wake up—we're in Delhi!"

We climbed out of the bus onto the bustling streets of Delhi. That day, we visited various rental houses. It was tough to find a cheap room , but eventually, we settled on a very small room We had to pay Rs. 3500 for a month's rent. Vaishnavi even tried to ask for a 10-day free trial but of course that doesn't make any sense.

I had planned to secure my spot at Saints Stephen College through sports quota. I had been playing cricket since I was a toddler and i had also captained my school team and since sports (especially for girls) are not very popular in India, the competition was relatively low. For getting a good college I shifted my hopes from Kota to to sports quota. I spent the following days practicing at various academies. You might wonder how I managed to afford cricket coaching—well, I used what I call the "Vaishnavi technique." In my experience, academies are far more likely to offer free trials than property owners are to do so.

<u>**9**</u>

On the day of the trial, I arrived at Saints Stephen College to give my cricket trial. After a decent interview, I made my way to the cricket field. I sat on a bench opposite the field to watch the game and waited for my turn. Judging by the level of the players, I felt confident that I could earn a spot at the college. I was better than most of the girls on the team, and when my turn finally came, I walked onto the field with confidence.

My first delivery was an outside off-stump ball. I let it pass—it was a wide. Kamini, the bowler I was facing, had good pace but poor line and length. The next ball was a sharp bouncer. I ducked to protect my head. I assumed it was a wide, but the umpire did not call it, so it was marked as a dot ball.

On the following ball, Kamini attempted a Yorker but missed the line. I flicked the ball lightly towards the boundary, and four runs were added to my score. The next few balls were uneventful, yielding only singles and doubles. At that point, I was on 9 runs from 10 balls and decided to accelerate my innings.

Then Shruti, a spinner, was given the ball. She bowled a top-spinner that hung in the air for a long time. Before it could touch the ground, I stepped forward and hit it with all my power. The ball soared high and far—it was a six! Our coach, Avinash Sir, gave me an appreciative look. On the very next ball, a frustrated Shruti bowled again, and I slammed it for a four. The following ball was good, and I drove it for a single, rotating the strike. In the next over, bowled by Kamini, I welcomed her with three consecutive boundaries.

I was batting on 46 runs from 32 balls when Priya, a fast bowler, struck me on the pads, and I was declared LBW by the umpire.

"How did it go?" Vaish asked as soon as I stepped into the house.

"Pretty well," I replied.

"I scored 46 off 33 balls."

"That's a good score—you'll probably get selected."

"Yeah," I said, settling onto a bed.

Later, Vaishnavi began counting the money she'd earned from her stories.

"Bhai, I got Rs. 2400 from writing for magazines," she said, showing me some crisp notes.

"I think I'll begin taking some home tuitions. We need more money," I said, lying down on the bed.

"I'll tell my parents when I get my admission letter from St. Stephen's," I added.

She sighed. "I'll tell my parents when I get employment," she said.

The next few days got pretty busy. Vaishnavi got a job as a teacher at a private school. At that time, there weren't many job opportunities for someone who had only completed their 12th grade. She had applied to be a journalist at a newspaper, but the newspaper didn't offer a specific job. She could write to them, and if they liked her articles, they would get published—that was it. On the other hand, the school was impressed by her literary skills and hired her as an English teacher. I started my tuition classes the day after the trial and began teaching a bunch of 6th graders how to multiply fractions, the Indus Valley Civilization, and how to separate husk from sand, among other things. Together, we made enough to survive peacefully in Delhi.

Every night, I would check my mail to see if there was an admission letter from St. Stephen's. A month passed.

"Akku, what would you tell your parents if you didn't make it to college?" she asked.

I had thought that out already.

"I'll say that I attempted JEE but failed to get in. I'll refuse to take a drop and start my business," I said, taking a bite of chapatti.

A silence followed. She sighed.

"I told my parents everything when you were taking classes today," she said.

I looked her in the eye, and by her look, I could tell it didn't end well.

"What happened?" I asked, concerned.

"Nothing much. I got a shouting from them. My mom said I was crazy. My dad said I had gone mad.

My mom said that writing is not a real occupation. I told them I was also teaching but they still disapproved. It's not like I'm doing a crime by writing stories," she said, taking a sip of water but it is OK we will manage without their support.

What are you supposed to reply to that? I tried to think of an answer that would calm her down. The room was filled with complete silence as I thought of a suitable response.

"I am here," I said, using the company's name.

There was a complete silence before Vaishnavi burst into laughter, and the room was filled with her infectious laughter.

<u>10</u>

I feel stupid for thinking I won't be able to make it to St. Stephen's. I mean, why wouldn't I? I laughed as I looked at my admission letter from St. Stephen's. I jumped in the air and shouted to Vaishnavi. We had gulab jamuns, a sweet Indian delicacy, to celebrate the feat. Then, amidst my happiness, I realized something.

Whenever something big happens, you have to remember all the things you said you would do if that thing happens. Sometimes these side thoughts are good; sometimes, they are terrifying. I reflected upon that as I dialed the number home. My heart beat was fast and itmatched the rhythm of the phone's rings. It was 4 heartbeats per ring, which is pretty fast. My mom picked up the phone after 20 heartbeats. (do the math yourself).

"Hi Mom, how are you?" I said, in a tone that felt like I had won the Nobel Prize or something. It's tough to shout at a happy person, especially fom moms. A part of them is always happy for you, even though they can be a little stern about IIT. You can be sure that their intention is always in your favor.

I never wanted IIT and ran away from Kota. I made it to St. Stephen's College, a prestigious institution," I said in one go. Okay, that was stupid. I should have broken the news slowly, but at that moment, I was carried by emotion and just wanted to be done with it. Done with hiding something. I just wanted to feel the relief of that moment.

"Wow," she said.

Okay, that was a really unexpected reply. I had never imagined a "wow" as a response. I mean, it was nice, but really unexpected.

"Which college?" Mom asked again.

I can't remember these Western names. Back in the day, there used to be Vidya Mandir College. Those were simpler times. And here she goes, talking about her favourite topic—old days.

In normal circumstances, I would have pointed out all the good things that have happened in this time, like the rise of feminism and gender equality.

But at that moment, I was just relieved that she wasn't shouting at me.

"Why did you choose that college? What's its name again?"

"St. Stephen's College, Mom, and it's a prestigious college. It matches my interests."

"Precisely, what's your interest?"

"Mom, I told you about my business idea. Remember?"

"You still have that?" she asked, as if she were asking, "Do you still have a fever after 5 days?"

"Yes, Mom," I replied.

"It's cool with me, but you know, you'll have to talk to your dad."

"Even if he doesn't approve, I'm not leaving the college. I've called you to give you the good news that I made it to St. Stephen's, and I'm pretty happy about it."

She was a little taken aback by my determination. I couldn't say she looked surprised because I couldn't see her face, but it seemed obvious. Anyway, after ending the call, I ran toward Vaishnavi. Well, I didn't actually run because there was hardly any space for running around in my house, but running means walking at your fastest speed, and I technically was moving toward her at my fastest speed under the circumstances. So, I can technically say I ran towards her instead of saying I moved toward her. But so basically, I ran toward her in the fastest way possible (just in case you still need clarification) and screamed, "I did it!"

<u>11</u>

I walked through the corridor of St. Stephen's College. It was full of excited newcomers and bored seniors who looked tired of showing students the way to the physics lecture room, the maths lab, or whatever. I found my way to the economics lecture room quite on my own.

I waited for something to happen. Soon, I was contributing to the noise in our lecture room. I wasn't exactly talking to anyone; we were just making noise.

The professor, Mr. Patel, entered the lecture room, and everyone turned silent. He was a tall man, over six feet with a muscular physique and a Hitler like mustache. I tried hard to control my laughter when he spoke **"Good morning, class,"** in a more feminine voice than any girl I knew. The voice awfully did not match his appearance. Anyway, the class began, and I found myself getting used to his voice, which sounded like it belonged to a 'her.'

"Suhani Verma."
"Present."
"Priya Aggarwal."

"Present."
"Kanika Joshi."
"Present."
"Arjun Sharma."
"Present."
"Jasdeep Bhullar."
"Present."
"Aisha Chauhan."
"Present."

I waited for my name as he took attendance. Finally, he said, "Akansha Trivedi."

"Present."

A boy looked at me. He seemed baffled, wearing an expression like he was at the end of a mystery. His look confused me. Why did he look like I was a puzzle he was trying to solve?

"Vikas Gupta."

"Present."

The boy answered.

I took in a sharp breath. I probably looked like I was at the end of a mystery too.

He was in the 12th grade when I last talked to him, so he should have been in his first year of college. He probably looked confused because he was doing some calculations in his head—wondering if I was the same Akansha he had helped escape from Kota.

The first class was just an introduction to economics. I found myself staring at Vikas more than once.

I found him looking at me more than once.

The class ended, and as we were exiting, I gathered my courage and asked, "Hey, Vikas, are you…?"

"Yes, I am a psychologist. Good to see that you did run away from that horrible place," he said and smiled. It was a charming smile.

"Yeah, thanks for that. It's so good to see you here. In the middle of strangers, it feels like finding gulab jamun between some fancy dishes. Not that these people are fancy, but they are just strangers… but gulab jamun hits different" I said, and we laughed together.

"For that, let's have gulab jamun in the canteen,"
he said and laughed.

Food makes good friends too.

<u>**12**</u>

Between Economics, Maths, and Computer Science, I spent a lot of time with Vikas.

We had only Economics in common.

He said he had opted for Economics to better understand human nature by seeing how people manage money. He wanted to be more than just a psychologist—he wanted to change the Indian mental health system. He wanted to push psychology beyond just polls and statistics.

Maybe that's what bonded us so strongly—the desire to change something.

I had told him that I would add mental health awareness to my curriculum, and then he had passionately told me about the importance of mental health.

Maybe it was this passion that brought us closer.

Except for economics, we also had a shared dream—to change something in this world.

Or maybe it was just our love for Indian food that got us closer. I don't know.

One day, we were walking around the college fields. Both of us had free periods, and we liked to spend them together. We walked silently. It was not an awkward silence—it was a comfortable silence, the kind only really close people can have.

I walked lightly, careful not to break the silence. It had just rained, and the soil smelled fresh. We were both staring at a solitary cloud in the sky; all the others had burst in the rain.

That's the thing about Vikas. You can talk to him for hours without getting tired, and you can also sit in silence with him without getting tired.

The silence turned more peaceful, more calming, and then he broke it by humming a tune. It was a soft melody flowing from his lips, the sound moving slowly in the air as if conscious of the melody it carried.

And then that last cloud burst open too.

We ran inside. Vikas was not much of an athlete—
he got tired halfway to the campus. He stopped,
and I stopped too.

We stood in the rain. Then he began sneezing, and
I laughed. And he laughed too.

Then we ran out of the rain.

I offered to drive him home, and we rode out of
the rain.

Only, we couldn't really drive out of the rain
because it was raining heavily near South Delhi,
where he lived. And we were on a motorcycle.

We were both going to catch a cold. I think he
already had.

But we were both laughing.

I dropped him at his house, , and then rode home
myself. On July 16th, I celebrated my first birthday
in Delhi. I've never been one to make a big deal out
of birthdays; to me, it's just the date I was born 19
years ago. I went to college as usual, entered my
economics class, and sat down at the third desk,
following my routine. Vikas approached my desk

and said, "Happy birthday! Have a wonderful day. Totally enjoy this day."

I never figured out how he knew it was my birthday.

I couldn't help but burst into laughter.

"Man, we are too big for these things," I replied.

"Are we too big to be happy? Come on, no one can ever be too big for celebrating a birthday. It's okay if you want to keep it simple, but you really should do the things you like," he responded.

"It's just a day I was born 19 years ago. Why celebrate it now?" I questioned.

He looked into my eyes and said, "We don't need reasons to be happy." Then he gave me a warm hug.

At that moment, it felt like time had stopped, as if we were the only people doing anything, and our embrace was the only thing happening in the world

Whenever there's nothing else, there's always cricket. We watched the World Cup match between India and Sri Lanka together. He was watching it at his house, and I at mine. We were connected on a call, discussing the match, cheering and cursing the same players, and telling each other not to move because Rohit was in his nineties. It's a good way to celebrate your birthday, but if India loses, don't blame me for spoiling your day. India won the game by 7 wickets, with 39 balls left, and made it to the World Cup semi-final, exiting the league stage as rank 1.

"The trophy is ours," Vikas declared as the Indian players walked out.

"New Zealand is not an easy team to defeat. They defeated us in the warm-up match of the World Cup, remember?" I said, turning off the TV.

"It was a warm-up game; this is the real match. We are number 1; they are number 4. We will win the semi-final and then the final ," he said with full confidence.

We were both standing tall during our national anthems as India faced New Zealand in the semi-final. There was more patriotism in the air than on Independence Day or Republic Day. Vikas was complaining that such big matches should be considered national holidays.

"But then other sports will get offended and feel discriminated," I countered. I knew, even without seeing him, that he was thinking, "Why can't they make other sports' big games national holidays too?"

New Zealand was batting first, and we were shouting the names of whichever Indian came to bowl, whether Bumrah or Bhuvi. Maybe it was the common passion for this beautiful game that brought us together.

"Bum bum Bumrah," he began shouting as Bumrah dismissed Martin Guptill.

"Guptill's role is over for this game," I said, not having a clue how wrong I was to be proven.

We never let them form any partnerships, except for the Williamson-Taylor stand. But I was so sure that India was going to win that I had already started wondering—who would India face in the final? England or Australia?

"What?!" he shouted just as it began to rain.

Soon, the covers were out, and we were staring at them.

"If this match is swept by rain, India will automatically qualify for the final, as India was above New Zealand in the league stage," I said.

"Then these people from New Zealand will cry for ages that they did not get a fair chance to defeat us. We will beat them fair and square," he said. "Rain, rain, go away. Come again another day. India wants to play. Rain, rain, go away."

We both began singing the nursery rhyme, modifying it a little to match the situation.

The whole day went like that. Rain would stop, the game would begin, then it would start raining again.

"I want this game to be won," he said, frustration dripping from his voice.

But we need not have worried. The ICC had kept the next day reserved just in case.

New Zealand was still batting when the game was postponed to begin the next day.

"It's not only the players who were bound to play another day; it is the two whole nations," I said, turning off the television.

We remained on the line even after the game was over. We mostly discussed tomorrow's approach and playing style, as if it would be us who would go to face New Zealand's dangerous bowling attack.

The next day began, and we played the national anthem again. Their batting was soon complete, and they gave us a target of mere 240.

`"Only Rohit can hit this much. This is not even a fight," Vikas spoke on the phone.

Rohit Sharma and KL Rahul's opening duo stepped out to bat; both of them had scored a century in the previous game.

Matt Henry to Rohit Sharma.

No, no, no.

And the batter who had scored five centuries in this World Cup was gone for a mere one.

"NO!" I screamed as I saw KL Rahul walk out of the pavilion for the same score as Rohit.

"We have Virat. We have Virat. We have Virat," was the only thing we could say at that moment of the game. We were so, so numb when we saw Virat go back to the pavilion for the same score. 5-3 looked like a terrible situation to be in—more terrible than you think.

"Switch off the stupid TV! This team is playing their stupid game in a stupid World Cup."

"No."

"We will see the whole game."

That's the thing about cricket. Until the result is declared, we never lose hope.

The pressure was so bad that Dinesh Karthik couldn't score even a single run in his first 20 balls. The pressure was so bad that I broke three pencils lying on the bedside table. The pressure was so bad that Vikas was smashing bats against the wall (thankfully, not the TV).

Soon, we lost Karthik on 6 off 23 balls. Pant and Hardik scored 32 each, but even then... we should have turned off the TV at 82-6. But Dhoni was around, and we did not.

"6!"

"It's a six! Jadeja is hitting sixes!" I said in amazement.

Then began the rain of boundaries. Jadeja was hitting them hard, and Dhoni was supporting him. Soon, we were dancing to the rhythm of Jadeja and Dhoni. That's the thing about cricket—just when you think it's over, it gives you hope. From 2%, the win probability rose to 44%. That's enough percentage for someone to cling to and fight for. That's enough percentage for a student to pass. That's enough percentage for it to break hearts when we saw Jadeja's wicket fall.

India was now 208-7 as Ravindra Jadeja got out on 77. We were both standing to give the man a big applause, but in fact, everyone had their eyes on a single man—Mahendra Singh Dhoni.

The six was enough for Vikas to begin dancing. It was big enough for us to feel hope. It was big enough for the whole of India to shout the man's name. It was big enough to make us completely, absolutely panic when he went for the risky double on the next ball.

"No. No. No! Dive! Dive, Dhoni, dive!" we shouted.

A direct hit from the same Martin Guptill ,whose role I had claimed to have been finished, was enough to shake us to the core. We knew Dhoni was gone even before the third umpire declared him out.

"OUT."

Three letters. Enough to break India's heart.

"Only rain can save us," I whispered. In a matter of one single day we had shifted from 'rain, rain go away' to 'Kaale Megha ,Kaale Megha paani to barsao'

The rain did come, but from both of our eyes.

Why did it even give us hope? We had accepted defeat at 82-6. Why was there a partnership?

Soon, India was bowled out for 221. I still did not have the heart to turn off the stupid TV. I was not hoping for Star Sports would announce that this match was a bad joke or some miracles like that. it was like i became addicted to a losing game. We were both crying silent tears.

This was the last One Day International of Dhoni.

This was the last match of India in this World Cup.

And something I did not know at that time—it was the last match Vikas and I watched together.

We were too heartbroken to watch the final of the World Cup. We were too heartbroken to play cricket in college. But life did not stop because of a match. But was this just a match played between two countries and 22 players, Or was it more than that?

There were exams in college. There were students to teach. I was sitting on my sofa, taking my last batch for the day. Soon, it was time for the students to walk back home. I had nothing much to do, so I took a stroll too.

I found myself in the streets, walking slowly in the humid air of July. The birds were going back to their homes, while I was doing the opposite. As I walked, I saw, in the dim light of the Delhi sun, a dozen kids playing cricket.

They did not know that with their plastic balls and bats, they were not just playing a game. They were filling us with hope.

A match can be lost, but the smiles I saw as these kids played could not be lost.

There would be light after dark.

There would be wins after losses.

And there would always be children playing in the streets, shining the days with hope and the sound of balls hitting bats.

And there would always be—

Light after darkness.

Wins after losses.

And always, children playing in the streets.

We were both sitting in the college canteen, talking slowly. "Do you think true love is a theoretical concept?" Vikas asked me, quite out of the blue. Cold September winds were blowing, making it the kind of day you crave hot chocolate. "As a girl who grew up reading Heer Ranjha and watching Veer-

Zaara, no, true love is not theoretical. It is one of the most real things ever noted by humans."

We began walking—I didn't know when. With Vikas, you don't have to make an effort for anything. You don't have to consciously start things. He has a sort of presence that makes you less conscious—or maybe so conscious that we forget everything else except what we were talking about.

"Do you think that people may believe it's true love when it's not actually true love?"

I paused a little and took a deep breath.

"What happened, Vikas?"

I could tell something was wrong by the way he asked his questions. I could tell something was wrong by the way he sighed. I could tell something was wrong by the way he kicked the stone near his foot.

He kept walking. "Just answer my question, Akansha. Please."

Name an astronaut to step on the moon. I asked him.

"Neil Armstrong."

"But how does it have to do with anything?"

So many astronauts have stepped on the moon after him, but he would still be the person you will first remember when I mention moon landing, because he proved to us that stepping on the moon is possible.

Like that, we can never forget our first loves, because they prove to us that we can love and be loved. That's why first love just takes a place in your heart, and even if it was not true love, you can never forget it, I said.

We walked together. We walked slowly.

He seemed to contemplate this for some time, and soon, there was another silence—a pensive one.

In which the only sound was of us walking and our feet touching the ground.

"What happened, Vikas?"

He remained silent, and we kept walking. He took a deep breath and almost whispered,

"My parents are getting divorced. Their love broke. They were pretending everything was okay, and then, it became difficult to act, and they got divorced."

I stared at him.

I didn't know how to reply to that, but maybe words don't matter that much. It is the feeling of support that matters. I hugged him tightly. Time stopped again. And then he was crying, and I was saying, "It's okay." And he was not trying to control his tears. He realized that there is no point in keeping tears in, there is no point in burying your sadness and suppressing your pain. I have a feeling that he knows this not because he has taken psychology training but because he knows it through experience.

Maybe the reason behind passions is your experiences—the way your life treats you.

I hugged him tight. He was sobbing now and said slowly, "Love is dead, Akansha. Love is dead."

I looked into his eyes, which were wet with tears.

"No. There is still love. Everywhere. It stands strong. There is love in the air and love in the sky. It is everywhere."

We were still walking. He was still sobbing. I hugged him again and whispered.

ou were saying love is dead, but here it is, Vikas, wrapped up in our embrace. Vikas, there is love. Vikas, I love you.

Sometimes, words don't matter. What matters are the feelings. Vikas did not say a word; he just hugged me tightly. It felt amazing to stand there in the college, hugging someone you love. We were both in a sort of trance. Among the wet eyes, there was love. I actually felt that there is love in the air, love in the sky, love everywhere.

It gave us an unreal sense of serenity and calm. My heart was not beating fast like when I was on a call with my mom. It was just relieved—the sort of relief you feel after coming home after a long day at work. I felt that with love, I had won the world. With love, there was also another component in the air and the sky—

Magic.

I had never felt the empty fields of our college so serene. I think it is not the places that are peaceful; it is the feelings, the emotions in our head that make all the difference. We walked back slowly to our respective classrooms because time had not stopped—it was us who had stopped for each other.

There are some things that words just cannot express.

Time had really not stopped. The shock of the divorce had hit his mom hard, and he flew back to Chhattisgarh to take care of her. When he was going back, I gifted him a diary.

It had **"It will be okay"** written on it. He hugged me and sat on the airplane. That was the last I saw of Vikas. I heard that he had left the college. I completed my graduation from Saint Stephen's and wanted to have some money before I started my business, so I became a math professor.

PRESENT DAY

I reread those messages again and again. I was purely lacking information. What happened to Vikas after he stopped talking? Why did he stop talking? Why did he leave Saint Stephen's? Why did he write those messages? I needed some sleep but could not get any. When somebody types gibberish, and you cannot even ask him why he wrote those, what does it even mean?

'Akansha,' calls out Vaishnavi.

'We will find him. We will find out everything that happened to him,' she says. I was in pure despair by then.

'Akansha,' she called out again, and I looked at her.

'We have to do something. We cannot let it be.'

'What can we do, yaar? How are we even going to ever find him? It is impossible.'

'Well, you are the brainy one,' she said and looked me in the eye.

'We will do it.'

It was late in the night, and I was tossing and turning in my bed. I seemed to have recovered a little from the shock of what happened. I was beginning to think a little. Suddenly, she knocked on my door. I opened it, and she entered with a triumphant look in her eyes, which I could make out even when the lights were off. She reflected it in her voice.

'I have an idea.'

There was no chance of sleep now as I was jolted by this revelation that there was a lamp in the dark.I felt the way I had felt seeing children play in the park that day.

'What is it?'

She laughed and said, 'You are so excited. You loved him a lot, no?'

'Shut up, Vais.'

'Okay, I will shut up and not tell you the idea,' she said and laughed again. She was clearly enjoying herself.

'Tell me the idea, man. Stop enjoying yourself.'

'Let me have some fun, man,' she said, smiling.

And the atmosphere was light-hearted again, as it is supposed to be when I and Vaishnavi are together.

'Okay, to be honest, it is not much of an idea, but it can be a good starting point. We can go to 'I Am Here's' official site and they may keep a record of their previous employees and the reasons they left. we can also talk to his colleagues

She smiled.

'I am not even sure if he left the company or not.'

I pulled out Vaishnavi's laptop and began typing. In a matter of seconds, I was dialing their customer service number.

'Bhai, it is midnight "

'If they don't pick up, we will call tomorrow, but we have nothing to lose,' I said.

'You really loved him a lot, didn't you?'

I was about to reply when the call was picked up.

'Hello?'

I was greeted by a masculine voice.

'Hello, this is Akansha. Is this from the I Am Here website?' I asked, my heart beating fast with excitement.

'Yes, this is Satvik. How can I help you?'

'Do you keep the record of past employees?' I asked, trying to sound calm. I failed miserably.

'Uhh... yes, but I can't give you the records.'

'I am looking to buy this business, and I really needed to get the data on who has worked here and your company, and I wanted to know employee satisfaction,' I said—the first thing that came to my mind. Vaishnavi gave me a mischievous smile and winked. She was trying hard to control her laughter.

There was a pause at the other end of the line.

'Uh, I think you should come to Lucknow. That is where our only branch is. You should talk to my seniors and the CEO, Arun Dutt. I simply lack the authority to talk about important matters like this,' he said, a little too politely to be natural.

'Alright, we would like to come to Lucknow,' I said and hung up the call. As soon as the phone was cut, both of us immediately began laughing.

'Was that the first thing that came to your instincts?' she asked.

'Well, I have billionaire instincts. I am destined to be the richest person on the planet, you know,' I said with my eyes twinkling.

<u>**13**</u>

We gazed at the blue sky from our window as the plane caught its flight. We were both wearing the most formal clothes we had, and we—well, still looked like jokers. I had practiced a formal smile, which I would definitely need while talking to Mr. Arun Dutt, the CEO. Satvik had informed his seniors about our arrival.

We gazed upon the clouds as we floated in the air. It felt quite different to act formal. I mean, the last time I wore these formal clothes was when I had interviewed at the Rani Lakshmibai College for my job. The best part about crazy things is how comfortably you can sleep when they're happening.

After all these years, I still rested my head on Vaishnavi's shoulder and dozed off.

I found myself being woken by Vaishnavi—I don't know how much time later.

"Bhai, wake up. You need to be active if you want to talk to the CEO," she said, giving me a water bottle she had bought from the airport.

I washed my drowsy face with some water and drank the remaining.

The flight landed in some time, and then we were walking out of the airport with confidence dripping from our faces. We booked the most expensive Ola, much to Vaishnavi's discomfort.

"Bhai, 800 rupees on a cab for a 15-minute ride? Have you gone crazy?"

"We have to look rich, and by the way, it's 785. Remember, we are potential buyers of a brand," I said, mischief dripping from my voice.

The car sped across the crowded streets of Lucknow. We were just minutes away from our destination when I abruptly stopped the driver.

"Yes, madam sahib?" he said in a UP accent.

I passed a 200-rupee note to him apart from the 785.

"Take this money and act like my personal driver, okay?"

He pocketed the notes and said, "And how exactly will I act like your personal servant, madam sahib?"

"Wait and watch," I said.

As we reached the head office, we were greeted by two ladies wearing formal smiles and clothing.

"Raju, park the car in the Poyo Hotel parking and stay in the room I have booked for you. I will tell you when I am free," I said.

Raju—if his name was that—looked genuinely impressed. I grinned from ear to ear, and so did Vaishnavi.

"Okay, madam sahib," he said and drove back.

We walked classily through the hotel. The two ladies showed us their office.

"You see those flowers? They are imported from California. We are a mental health startup, and these flowers are good for the mental peace of our employees."

"Oh, that's great. Nice," I said.

"We have blue curtains, madam. They are really good for stress management as blue represents tranquillity and trust."

"What's the music?" asked Vaishnavi.

The lady looked excited, like she wanted her to ask that question.

"Madam, these are binaural beats. They increase the focus of our brain and help employees stay focused. They are scientifically designed to correspond to the wavelengths of our brain to help maintain focus."

"How scientific," I said.

This woman had really prepared well, and it would be good to please her, I thought.

"Madam, what's your name? We would definitely like to give you a promotion if we come into possession of this business," I said.

She looked really excited at the prospect of making connections with rich people and maybe her future boss's boss's boss.

"My name is Nandini, and I have worked here since this business started," she said, extending her hand for a handshake.

"Nice to meet you, Nandini. Before talking to the seniors, I would like to ask you—what is the mechanism of this business?" I asked in an unforced manner.

I had grown a liking to the enthusiastic Nandini, who worked in I.A.H.

"We have three types of employees here," she began.

"One—psychologists. Two—AI programmers. And three—finance managers. There are also some people like me, who are receptionists, greeting people who comes here. The CEO of the psychologists is Sarvika Mehta, and she keeps a record of how many psychologists work here and which accounts are assigned to whom. All the psychologists work from home, and they only come to the office on the 2nd and 4th Saturdays of the month. On those days, they are given training on how to talk to clients and how to enhance their experience. All the other employees are on leave on those days," she said and took a pause.

"I want to talk to Miss Sarvika. Where is she?" I asked.

"It was nice talking to you, Nandini."

"Miss Sarvika's office is on the upper floor. Let me guide you there."

"Sure," I said as we climbed the stairs along with Nandini.

We were guided into a cabin.

"Miss Sarvika Mehta" was written in bold letters on a nameplate.

"Good morning, ma'am. I am Akansha Trivedi, and this is Vaishnavi Chouhan. We are here to talk to you about this startup," I said in a confident tone. It seemed like even my subconscious had accepted that I was here to buy this startup.

"I am Sarvika Mehta, and I lead the psychologist unit in this startup," she said in an even more confident voice as we shook hands.

"So, Sarvika, tell me—what is the work culture here with psychologists? I really expect honest answers," I asked like I was genuinely interested.

"There are no specific work hours for psychologists in I.A.H. They get 1000 rupees per account they take in per month. They can take as many accounts as they like, but they have to reply to any customer request made during the time periods of 9 AM to 6 PM."

Suddenly i was hit by a revelation that Vikas was working overtime that day when I messaged him at midnight.

In the middle of that meeting, I was lost in his thoughts. I had trouble concentrating on what Sarvika had to say. I just wanted to text him. I just wanted to talk to him, and that's what I was here for.

If I wanted to talk to him, I needed to get clues. I needed to talk to his boss and colleagues.

As a psychologist, he would have only come on the 2nd and 4th Saturdays.

With a jerk, I realized that tomorrow would be the 2nd Saturday of the month, and if I came again the next day, I would get a chance to talk to his colleagues and maybe get a few details.

"We would like to talk to some of your psychologists. Nandini told me that they only come on the 2nd and 4th Saturdays. Since tomorrow is the 2nd Saturday of the month, we will come again tomorrow if you don't mind," I said and looked at Sarvika.

"Why would we have any problem? We would welcome you any day, ma'am," she said.

I mentally high-fived Vaishnavi. I did some Ronaldo-style 'Suis' in my head as I ended my meeting and walked out of the cabin.

Later That Night

I rested on the bed after a hectic day. I had stayed in the office for two more hours after talking to Sarvika, I even managed to talk to Arun Dutt - the CEO for a while. I had even managed to talk with some other employees. At some point, the topic of me buying **I.A.H** came up, but I firmly stated that I would only make a decision after talking to the psychologist unit.

Then they offered us dinner. We indulged in paneer tikka, korma, and Lucknow's special veg kebabs. We also had veg biryani with delicious raita. And for dessert, they even had my favorite—gulab jamuns.

After returning to our room, we decided to walk instead of taking an expensive cab ride since we had already had a heavy meal. Slowly, we made our way to the hotel we had booked.

Back in the comfort of our room, Vaishnavi opened her laptop and tried to write something.

"Why are you playing beats on your keyboard?" I asked as she tapped the rhythm of a song on the keys.

"Bhai, I can't concentrate. For the first time in years, my life seems more interesting than the novel I'm typing," she said, continuing to tap out a beat of the song 'APT' using the Shift and Control keys.

I pulled out my phone and found myself staring at Vikas's contact info. I reread those messages over and over again.

Somebody betrayed him. And during this difficult time in his life, he texted me.

That too, when we hadn't exchanged a single word in over six years.

If Lucknow were a small city, I would have gone street to street, asking people about Vikas Gupta. Maybe if nothing worked, I would try that.

But I seriously hoped something would work in this wild goose chase.

Then, after quite some time, my thoughts drifted to my dream of changing the education system.

I had never felt any passion for college-level trigonometry, which I now taught daily. What was I doing? I had become a professor just to raise money for my business, but I had never actually worked on turning my fantasy into an action plan.

Had Vikas accomplished his dream of starting a mental health business?

I remembered how we were both passionate about passion itself. That, I think, had brought us close in the first place.

Before I knew it, I found myself searching for "Vikas Gupta" on Google.

A million Vikas Guptas appeared in front of my eyes. None of them was **my** Vikas Gupta.

Then, I smiled—because I had never thought of Vikas as mine before.

But he wasn't mine now either.

And so, I found myself typing...

Vikas Gupta mental health startup.

I stared at the screen for a long, long time. Seeing his face—even on the screen—made the hair on my body stand up. A torrent of emotions flooded my head, and I didn't know which one to acknowledge. Then, like a teenager, I found myself checking his marital status.

To my relief, I found out that he was unmarried.

Then, I saw a picture of him with someone I recognized. I stared at the other man for a long time, and then it hit me—I had seen him today. It was **Arun Dutt**, the CEO of I.A.H.

Friends are like F.M. Sometimes, they can sometimes act as Google Maps too. But sometimes, they can become the destination itself. I called out to Vaishnavi immediately.

"Vaishnavi, come here!" I shouted, my tone making it clear that my heart was beating faster than the Vande Bharat train.

I told her everything I had found, and she snatched the phone from me. She, too, seemed to care about it as much as I did at that instance. I was filled with warmth just by the fact that all of this mattered to her.

"The co-founders of Mental Mentor are Vikas Gupta and Arun Dutt," she read aloud.

It was my turn to snatch the phone back. I stared at Vikas. His smile looked so natural, so sweet. The mission he had chosen for himself really mattered to him.

I couldn't take my eyes off that smile.

I had never thought that I would see that dazzling, genuine smile again. But here I was, gazing at it. I ignored the fact that it was just a picture, accessible to anyone on the internet. I ignored the fact that I hadn't seen him in more than five years. I just felt happy. Happy that he had shared his dream with me before the world.

I liked to believe that it was something personal. I liked to think that I even knew the backstory of this business—how he had witnessed mental instability in his parents' marriage, and how that had transformed an idea into a passion.

I imagined him typing my name into Google and feeling disappointed that I had done nothing worthwhile with my dreams, my passion.

"Vikas and Arun worked together. He can give us crucial details about Vikas," Vaishnavi said, waking me from my reverie.

At that moment, I just felt so grateful to have her around during one of the most confusing phases of my life. Vaishnavi isn't the kind of person who fades from my thoughts when I think about Vikas. Over the past six years, I never had the heart to ignore her. Our bond had gone beyond friendship—it had become something much stronger.

With her, I had made memories for life—running away from Kota, meeting Vikas, and now this web of mysteries I found myself entangled in.

Then, I realized that I had been wrong when I said the crazy events in my life had no common link between them.

I realized that, apart from Vaishnavi, there was one single thing connecting them all.

Actually, not a thing. A man.

Vikas.

<u>15</u>

I sat on a rocking chair, facing **Arun Dutt**, the CEO of **I.A.H** and the co-founder of **Mental Mentor**.

We had spent an hour talking to the psychology unit, and we had received the same information—Vikas had left **I.A.H** and had worked with Arun Dutt to create another mental health company called **Mental Mentor**.

We hadn't received any more information, however.

All our cards were stacked on this meeting now.

"So, since you've spoken to the psychology unit, can we begin negotiations now? This company is a rising startup, and I believe its estimated value would be around 50 crores," Arun said, looking at me expectantly.

I responded with another question.

"Sir, after speaking with the psychology unit, we found that you, along with **Vikas Gupta**, own another mental health startup called **Mental**

Mentor. We are also interested in that startup and would like to know more details about it. We would also like to speak with Mr. Vikas."

I said this confidently.

"Sure, ma'am. I'll tell you about how it works," Arun said. "It's basically a company with several purposes. It educates people about mental health and how to improve it. It also organizes seminars where famous personalities talk about mental health, which we record and publish. This increases awareness and helps build trust."

"People in India rarely seek psychologists because they don't trust strangers with their personal issues. But when they see well-known personalities discussing their struggles, it builds credibility.

We also have a team of professional psychologists, and we offer a course—not just to train new psychologists, but also to help people master their own mental health and find happiness.

Our long-term goal is to make psychology a part of the school curriculum. We are also in discussions with education boards and government officials to address fundamental issues affecting mental health in India, such as toxic work culture and the immense pressure of examinations," he said proudly.

"That is fascinating and has the potential to change India," I said. "We are really interested in this, but I believe it is essential to talk to **Vikas Gupta**. I want him to participate in the negotiations. Since the decision to sell or not sell the businesss controlled by both of you, this will also ensure there are no legal complications."

I saw Arun's expression changing.

"Ma'am, I'm afraid that won't be possible at this moment. I haven't been able to contact him myself. I went to his house, and it was locked. But more baffling was the 'For Sale' board on his property."

He hesitated before continuing.

"It seems like he has disappeared," he said nervously, as if fearing that this revelation might break the deal.

I took a sharp breath and sighed.

I had expected this.

It was clear from his messages that he was keeping something to himself and it was only logical that he didn't tell Arun either.

"It's not a big problem," Vaishnavi suddenly spoke, breaking her silence. "Just tell us his address, and we'll take care of the rest. We are really interested in your company, and we'd like to clinch a deal. We'll manage this issue as well."

Arun looked hesitant for a moment.

Then, probably after making some mental calculations, he came to the conclusion that giving us Vikas's address wouldn't cause him any harm.

"He lives in Shri Ram Dass Colony, near the Head Post Office. I don't know his exact address, but you'll easily find him," he said, shaking hands with us.

We walked out of the cabin, knowing that we had nailed this meeting.

And that **Vikas** was not as far away as he had seemed four days ago.

Shri Ram Dass Colony was too small to have more than one house with a "For Sale" board and **'Gupta'** on the nameplate.

We were now standing in front of a blue-gated, 26 by 56 house.

It felt good to stand there.

I felt **close** to him at that moment.

And I **smiled.**

I felt hopeful.

I contemplated the possibility of seeing him.

We knew what we had to do.

We rang the bell of the house adjoining Vikas's.

A woman in her mid-50s opened the door.

"Yes?" she asked, looking us up and down.

"We are interested in buying the neighboring house. Do you know which property dealer the owner might have contacted? Or who the owner is?" I asked.

Now, there are a lot of disadvantages to being a woman in India.

But there is one advantage.

No one suspects you of being a criminal.

"Uh, Vikas Gupta lived here. He was about 25. He must have contacted Kirpal Singh, he's a famous real estate agent in this area. He only got us this house we are living in," she said before providing us the contact details of both Vikas and Kirpal. I had hoped that this number of Vikas's would be different from the one I had, but it turned out not to be. However, we still had the phone number of Kirpal Singh.

I thanked the lady and dialled the number of Kirpal Singh. The phone rang, and my heart beat four times per ring again, just like it did on the day I called my mom to tell her about Kota. He picked up the call after the sixth ring, or 24 heartbeats.

"Hello," came the deep voice, with a mixed Lucknavi and Punjabi accent.

"Sir, we wanted to buy the house owned by Vikas Gupta in Ram Das Colony. Has he registered the house to you?" I asked. Vaishnavi looked at me, confused. I had not yet told her about my plan. I grinned from ear to ear. I was certainly enjoying myself.

My plan was simple. We just had to go inside his house under the pretext of checking the interiors as prospective buyers, and once inside, look for any clues.

"Yes, ma'am, he registered his house to me for selling."

"Do you have the key? We are standing in front of the house and would really like to see the interiors," I asked, enjoying the amused look on Vaishnavi's face as she finally got my plan.

"Sure, madam, I'm coming in 20 minutes," he said and cut the call.

"Bhai, you are crazy," she said as she took a bite of bhutta she had just bought from a vendor.

"That I am," I said, snatching her bhutta and eating it myself.

"This is the living room, and this is the first bedroom on the first floor," said Kirpal as we explored Vikas's house. He had arrived in exactly 20 minutes, and after shaking hands with us, he began showing off the house. He was now showing us the interiors of the house.

I sneaked out of the living room and began entering room to room to find clues. I stood there staring at the book rack. I never knew that he read books. I walked closer towards the bookcase and found that there were sticky notes over every bundle. I read all of those.

"Young adult novels. Mystery stories. Psychological stories. Historical novels. Self-help books. Fantasy stories. Stories about true love."

I examined the book rack more closely and found that two books were not part of any column. I held them in my hands to examine them. Then, I realized that both of them had the same wording as their title: *It Will Be Ok*.

I realized with a flash that they were diaries, and I had gifted one of them myself. I leafed through the pages, and they were filled with his handwriting. I realized that I could find so much about Vikas if I just simply read his journals. I stuffed them in a small bag I was carrying and kept looking. I tried to look for any electronic device which could have stored some data, but found none. After properly examining the house, I climbed down the stairs and signaled to Vaishnavi that I had found something.

"About how much will I expect to get for the house?" she asked. I don't know why.

"About 80 lakhs, ma'am. The owner has told me not to contact him and just sell the house at anything above 80," he said.

"Not more than 55," I said, just to make conversation and look genuine, like I had come for the sole purpose of buying it.

"Ma'am, there is no scope for bargaining. I can't even talk to the owner."

"It's too expensive, totally out of budget," I said, and we walked away.

As soon as we were away from the earshot of Kirpal, Vaishnavi asked, "What did you find?"

"His journals," I said, smiling as we walked toward our room.

As soon as we reached our room, I settled down in my bed and began reading the diaries. I felt a little guilty while reading his personal stuff, but I knew I had to read this, and it began just from where we had left off.

September 2, 2019

"There is something magical about first love," she said. I wanted to tell her that she was mine. My life seems like an uninterrupted riddle. After their divorce, I am just speechless. But I am not shocked. I would have imagined myself to feel numb at this situation, but I am not. I am feeling emotion. I always tell my distressed clients to make a list of what emotions they feel, and this is mine:

1. Grief because of the divorce.
2. Confusion because of the mess. And last
3. Unconditional and uncontrollable love for her.

September 28 , 2019

I had to extend my leave from college because my mother is very ill. The worst part is that dad didn't even come to see her when she was admitted to the hospital. I believe this has broken mom more than anything, and I can almost feel her emotions right now. Her pure soul would not feel anger for my dad; she would just be thinking maybe it was all her fault, and I know somewhere or the other, about something or the other, she would be feeling guilt. I want to tell her that it was not her fault. I will tell her that when the hospital staff allows me to meet her, that is. My extended leave means that I don't get to see Akansha for some more time now. I want to tell her a lot of things. I want to tell her my feelings for her and how grateful I am to her for supporting me. But most of all, I want to hear her talk. I want to hear her cheerful voice, and I want to float in the air after listening to it. Love is really a great feeling.

September 29, 2019

My mom got out of the hospital today. I am leaving for Saint Stephen's in two days. And yes, I did tell her that it was not her fault. She hugged me after that and began crying. I was soon in tears too. Crying is a thing I was never ashamed of. I always believe in emotion. I believe in grief as much as I believe in love. God, I can't even write a few sentences without thinking about her. I hope to see her soon.

March 4, 2020

I am writing in this diary after about half a year now. You know why? Because I was in jail. My colleague—Ajeet Singh recently got murdered. I was too shocked, and then the police began accusing me of his murder, as I visited his house that day. I couldn't even cover the shock of his death when they put me in jail for his murder. And that news was all over the newspapers. My mom was so tensed and sad that she found herself in a hospital again. I felt so awful that day. Those days were the worst part of my life, and now I just don't want to face Akansha. She would think of me as a murderer, even though I am proven innocent. But if you once think someone is a murderer, you can't be close to them. I left Saint Stephen's too. I don't want to go back to that college. I am not the Vikas I used to be. I have changed so much. I even left I.A.H, but that was not a burst of emotion. That was because I want to pursue the dream. Maybe if I am successful in that dream, maybe I can face her again. Tomorrow is my meeting with Arun Dutt, the CEO of I.A.H. I want to talk to him about Mental

Mentor. I want to start that with him. I need his expertise, and I know I will make a good pair with him.

Mental Mentor has an attachment for her hidden in it. I told her about it, and she knows it. I hope that I am successful in the meeting with Arun Dutt tomorrow. Funny how a hopeless passage ends with an 'I hope so'. I read that at the bottom of the last letter I had written that I hope to see her soon, but I cannot stop hoping for it; it has kept me alive in this mess that I am in.

March 5, 2020

You miss people the most on the days when something big happens in your life. Today was such a day for me. I could not get her out of my head all day. I went to I.A.H, but not as an employee. I was there to have a meeting with its CEO. His secretary told me to wait for 5 minutes. Those 5 minutes turned into more than 2 hours. I sat there, observing things. As I sat in the office reception, I heard the binaural beats—the music which was said to help us focus. My thoughts drifted away to Akansha again. I realized that she was my background music, the one making me focus on my dreams. She was the one who was unknowingly keeping me fighting on the battlefield. She was my background music, keeping me motivated to walk through the scorching days of my life. In some time, I found myself sitting in front of Arun Dutt. I told him about Mental Mentor. I told him everything I had crafted about it in all these years. He asked me a few questions. I answered all of them confidently. If you have thought about something for seven years before going to sleep, it would be difficult for Arun to present any problem whose answer I didn't already know.

By the end of the meeting, we were shaking hands and planning our business inauguration date. For the first time in quite a lot of time now, I smiled a genuine smile, knowing that I was on the right track.

June 5 , 2020

Don't worry, I am writing after a lot of time, not because I found myself in jail or terrible stuff like that. I was just so caught up in work all the time. Just after we launched our business, the world was hit by a terrible pandemic, COVID-19. The whole of India was in lockdown mode, and Arun and I were able to execute the online app for Mental Mentor.

We were also able to convince people that during the COVID pandemic, keeping your mental health stable is the key to staying fit. We were able to connect with some hospitals, and we provided free counselling to get out of depression to the families who had lost a family member to COVID. Arun said that it would make a good public figure for our brand, which was crucial for working in a country like India, which had not yet begun trusting the importance of mental health and was always skeptical about it. If you ask me how I feel, I just feel happy.

You may be wondering why I write these diaries like i am talking to someone. Well, I just can't shake the feeling that somebody is reading these diaries, or will one day. So hello, whoever is reading.

<u>16.</u>

I was in tears by then. I kept his diary aside and wiped them away. That was too much to process at once. I managed to somehow control my tears when i reached the binaural beats part, but this time, i couldn't. It has always been my habit—i never cry at the most difficult times, but the dam i store inside bursts suddenly, and then there is no stopping it. I realized i was suffering from information and emotional overload. I needed to stop reading and reflect. I left the diaries and went out for a walk, wandering through the crowded streets of lucknow, thinking.

I didn't even know that Vikas was an accused murderer. I loved him. I love him. Does he still love me? I thought. Based on the messages he sent, it certainly seemed so. The messages—what was the reason he sent them? Then i realized that i needed to read more. I couldn't think about anything else except him at that moment. So, i turned and began walking back to my room. I couldn't live without knowing. I couldn't love without knowing.

AUGUST 7, 2020

Mental Mentor is growing rapidly now. We are making good profits and, more importantly, changing the mental health situation in India. We plan to approach the Government of India to limit the maximum working hours of an individual, even if they are working in the private sector. But we can't do that yet, as we haven't gained enough power and influence. When we do have everything in our favor, we will also try to improve the education system in India, especially in terms of mental well-being for students.

She also wanted to change the education system. She also thought that the Indian education system needed a lot of improvement. She would be in her second year now. Sweet Akansha, I don't think she ever went away from my life. I can feel her presence. She has become a part of me. They weren't lying when they said that love changes people. I don't remember who said it, but it must be someone wise.

I now know that true love isn't just a theory. It's as real as you and me. It's as real as me and her.

AUGUST 18,2022

I never thought that I would fall in love.

I never thought that I would get separated from my love. I thought my only love would be The Mental Mentor.

But here I am, missing Akansha. There were 53 students in our class. In every sports period, the children would make pairs and teams with even numbers of players, but the total number of stdents was 53. I would always be left out—would always fail to be a part of a team. At the beginning of every session, I would pray for a new admission to come, to make the numbers even so that no one felt left out.

It never did. Roll number 54 never came. That's when I decided I would create a mental health startup—so that if anyone ever felt alone, he or she could come to therapy. I wanted to be roll no. 54 for people.

To provide them support, company, and maybe even friendship. Joining IAH was supposed to be my first step toward being roll no. 54.

I never, in my wildest dreams, imagined that I would find the person I had wanted all my life there.

I never thought I would find Akansha—my roll no. 54. Now, roll number 54 or the background music may not feel romantic to you,

but my friend, they do to me.

They do to me.

AUGUST 27, 2020

I am still in shock over what happened. It just happened too quickly for me or anyone to react. Everything was fine yesterday, and suddenly, out of nowhere, I found myself standing at my mother's funeral pyre. Cardiac arrest, I'm told by Dr. Rajan Manmohan, but I'm too dazed to react. I feel like my life is breaking into tiny fragments, and so is my heart. I'm still too numb to react, and I feel emotionally exhausted more than anything.

I still can't believe it all happened. I desperately want to talk to someone, but it seems like I have no one left. My mom is gone and Akansha is distant, and I am completely dazed. I'm not close enough to Arun to confide in him about my feelings, as our relationship is strictly business. So, I write to you, mysterious person. And Akansha gave me this diary, and in a way, I am connecting to her too. I really needed to share my emotions with someone, so thank you, mysterious person, for listening. And thank you, Akansha, for giving me this dear mysterious person.

2 JANUARY , 2021

The way I express my life after my mom's death is through work, work, and more work. I realized that the only company I have now is Mental Mentor, my life's mission. So, I hold on to it for support. It's also the only way I can still reach Akansha. More than a year has passed since I lost touch with her, and I still can't get over her. I seriously need closure. It's like you were at the climax of a movie, and then there's an electricity cut. You can't think about anything except that movie.I really miss her, and my mom, my dad—everyone I am losing so rapidly.

Arun helped me get through my mom's death. I can now talk to him like a buddy or a close friend. I seriously need his support, and I strongly appreciate it. I haven't told him about Akansha though. I just want her thoughts to be mine and mine alone.

AUGUST 9 , 2021

Mental Mentor has grown a lot since I last wrote. It is now a proper company with employees. As COVID has decreased quite a lot, we also function offline. We got 24 famous Indian psychologists, paid them well, and had them train people in psychology. We hired all those people to teach mental awareness to the entire country. We've opened 5 branches—one in Lucknow, Delhi, Patna, Noida, and Kanpur. Our online courses and classes are also being purchased and implemented by a lot of Indians. We hope to gain enough power by the end of this year to make a change in the Indian education system. She would be so proud.

4 November 2022

I am writing after a long time, and I have Mental Mentor to thank for that. I live happily now, even though I still miss Akansha. But you know, when a fantasy you've held onto for half your life seems to come true, it's hard to remain sad, isn't it?

Today, I find myself thinking about her more than usual. We had our meeting with the education minister, and we were able to make a small difference—we successfully pushed for a reduction in syllabus and for schools to emphasize that exams are not everything. Failing an exam doesn't mean you are incapable; you can always come back stronger, whether in academics or another field, as long as you work hard. Although the impact was small, it gave me immense satisfaction.

I had an urge to call her and tell her about it but didn't. It's weird to pop back into someone's life after three years. Instead, I pictured how she might look now, and after the image formed in my mind, I couldn't help but smile.

We have more meetings lined up, and I hope we can improve India's toxic work culture. We will try our best—I swear we will.

6 November 2022

We had our meeting yesterday with some government officials, but they rejected all our suggestions for improving work culture. I tried to explain that reducing working hours could actually increase productivity, but those idiots didn't have the ears for it. Bloody rascals.

OCTOBER 8,2024

Writing in this journal after a really long time. I only write here when I feel the need to.

These days, I'm working a lot with Arun Dutt to make Mental Mentor a household name. We're paying YouTubers for advertisements, hiring ten employees just for social media marketing, and joining multiple Facebook groups focused on mental health. We first contribute valuable discussions and, over time, introduce Mental Mentor to these communities. We've also created our own Facebook group, where we regularly post about mental health while promoting our platform. Our team uploads shorts and reels on platforms like YouTube and Instagram, and we're planning to hire more people for offline marketing as well.

I'm still single, but I have good friends. I've grown very close to Arun—he's almost like a brother to me now. He recently got married. Everyone keeps telling me to settle down too, but I don't want to marry or even date anyone.

I know the person who gave me this diary plays a big role in why I don't want to fall in love again. I still think about her—only sometimes, maybe once a month. Okay, maybe once a week. Fine, once a day, but no more, I promise.

I want to contact her in a few months. I really want to catch up with her. And apologize for not talking to her for so long. Sometimes, I feel guilty about that. I know it was a mistake, but everyone makes mistakes, and at that time, I was completely broken and hopeless.

She is still a big reason I work so hard for Mental Mentor. She is still, after all these years, my binaural beats.

5 January 2025

Everything. Everything is lost.

My hands are shaking as I write this.

I said I wanted to contact her—I did. But not under these circumstances.

Okay, I'm not making sense right now, but life isn't making any sense either.

Let me start from the beginning of this mess.

I was at Arun's house, and we were discussing strategies to scale Mental Mentor. I got up to use the wash room, but on my way, I spotted bundles of drugs. At first, I was too shocked to react. I just stood there, frozen.

Arun came looking for me and saw that I had seen the drugs. The moment he realized that, he lunged at me and started punching me. Somehow, I managed to break free and run. Then the bastard took things to another level—he pulled out a gun and started shooting at me. Only I know how I managed to escape.

But he wasn't done. He kidnapped my close friend Ajay and threatened to kill him if I told anyone.

I decided to leave India. I'm going to Finland's capital city. It's the happiest country in the world. Maybe there, I can find something for myself.

But even now, I feel nothing. No anger. No sadness. Not even betrayal. I think my senses are shutting down. My emotional mind hasn't processed what happened yet.

I realized there was no one I could trust. I had lost everything, everyone.

And then I thought of you.

I had always felt like Akansha was reading this. She was the mysterious person turning the pages of my life.

So I told her—I told her I was leaving for Finland, even though I didn't explain why.

But why am I not escaping? Why am I writing all this in a diary?

Listen, Akansha, I can't live with the thought that no one cares for me. So, I am wishing—praying—that you do. Somehow, if manage to get Arun in jail i will know that you care and my messages matter to you.

I am in the capital city of Finland. If he is behind bars and everything is safe, meet me there.

Bye.

I love you.

The diary ended there. but that was not the only thing that ended. The confusion about the messages he sent ended too.

It was clear now—he still loved me, even after all these years.

I read the last line over and over. My heart filled with rage for Arun Dutt. At that moment, I could have killed the bastard myself.

There was a tsunami of emotions inside me, and I felt them all.

I felt the most powerful force in the world, from the world's most powerful emotion—love.

And when you're in the throes of unconditional love, you don't just feel love. You feel everything associated with your love story.

I felt an overwhelming hatred for Arun—so intense that my blood boiled. So intense that Vaishnavi noticed something was wrong just by looking at my face.

"Akku, what happened?" Vaishnavi asked, looking me straight in the eyes.

I handed her the diaries. It was something I couldn't put into words. I couldn't explain it—I wanted her to feel the emotions directly from their source. Okay, maybe I didn't want her to feel love for Vikas, but apart from that, I wanted her to experience everything I was feeling.

Then I realized—there were two diaries, not just one. I picked up the other diary, opened the first page, and began reading.

"Akansha, maybe it's not as easy as I thought for you—or anyone—to put Arun in jail. He has released Ajay, my friend whom he held hostage, on the condition that I won't say a word to anyone. If you can't do it, it's ok.

But hey, Akansha, I love you. And it's fine if you don't feel the same way. After all, it's been a long time since we last spoke. I want you to somehow find these diaries then I would know you care.

Remember how I once said that, as a psychologist, I would advise you to stay positive and make the best of your time in Kota, but as a friend, I would tell you to leave?

Well, now, as a psychologist, as a friend, as a lover—I'm telling you to follow your dreams. The satisfaction I felt after bringing even a small change was incredible. So incredible that I want you to feel it too.

Give it your best, Akansha. Never give up on your dreams. And most of all, never give up on yourself.

Keep this diary as a reminder of what you dream of.

And maybe, just maybe, give me a chance to be your background music."

"No, Vikas. It's not difficult to get Arun in jail. And I still love you. I thought I didn't, but I felt it after you sent those messages. I'm here for you, Vikas.

And yes, I will finally start working on my dreams— I have been thinking about them a lot lately—once the Arun mess is sorted, I'll come to Finland. I want to see you so much.

And then, maybe, you can finally match your imagination with how I look now.

See you soon.

I love you."

After pouring my heart out, I felt a level of motivation I had never experienced before.

Vaishnavi was still reading the diary, and I had nothing else to do. I glanced at the time—it was 7 in the evening. That's when I realized how hungry I was.

I ordered Dal-roti from Zomato. I needed my comfort food after such an exhausting and emotional day.

As I waited for my food and for Vaishnavi to finish reading, I sat by the window and felt myself floating back to my old fantasy.

The fantasy I was now determined to fulfill.

Then, without a second thought, I opened my laptop.

There was research to be done to start the business.

<u>17</u>

The food arrived shortly, and we both dug into the comforting combination of dal and chapatis cooked to perfection. We didn't speak a word throughout the meal. We were too busy lost in our thoughts. As soon as we finished eating, Vaishnavi picked up the diaries and continued reading. I saw her cheeks turn pink with rage, and her breathing became erratic. She had a shocked expression on her face.

"It was Arun, that rascal. Now the police will buy his business, idiot!" she shouted as she finished reading.

"Relax, girl. He'll soon be behind bars," I reassured her.

"Yeah," she said, gulping down some water. Her expression softened, and she looked at me with a mischievous smile. "Vikas Jiju is in Finland then, and he loves you."

"Shut up," I said, my cheeks turning red as I blushed. True love really isn't theoretical.

<u>18</u>

I woke up the next day to find our whole room in disarray, with Vaishnavi searching for something ruthlessly in my room.

"Where are those diaries?" she asked as soon as she noticed I was awake.

"I kept them at the bedside table near my bed," I replied, still half-asleep.

"Yes, but they're not there."

"It doesn't matter; we've already read them," I said. "Get up and prepare. We need to talk about buying the business. Remember?" she added with a crooked smile.

"But we won't take an Ola today. We'll rent a motorbike," she said.

"Huh, why?" I asked, puzzled.

"They already believe we're rich, and we need the bike. I'll explain the significance later," she replied, as we walked out of our hotel. She hopped onto the driver's seat or whatever it is called on a bike, and we raced towards I.A.H Headquarters to confront the culprit.

She took a different route, and since we weren't familiar with the area, we followed Google Maps' instructions. She parked the bike in an unconventional spot, and I eyed her suspiciously. But we didn't have to wait long before we were escorted by Nandinii to Arun's office. She closed the door behind us as we entered his cabin. Soon, it was just me, Vaishnavi, and Arun in the room.

"You think you're too clever?" Arun began. "You want to play detective with me?" He picked up his rifle.

I gasped, but Vaishnavi didn't seem surprised. I gasped again as I saw Vikas's diaries lying on the table.

Was Vaishnavi behind it all? I wondered, glancing at her, but she wasn't looking at me. She jumped and kicked him hard in the stomach. Blood spilled out as he groaned in pain.

"Follow me," she said, opening a door I hadn't noticed before. As we stepped out, our bike was waiting for us. We got on and started riding.

"I knew this would happen," she said as the bike picked up speed. "That's why I rented the bike and parked it here. If we had to escape, we wouldn't waste time looking for it a kilometer away or waiting for a cab."

"The police station is just a 3-minute ride from here. I took the other route so we wouldn't need to look for it," she added, panting.

I felt stupid for ever doubting my best friend. I wanted to hug her at that moment.

She stopped the bike at the police station, and we walked inside.

"How can I help you?" the inspector asked, gesturing for tea.

"We think Arun Dutt, a businessman and owner of I.A.H company, is a drug dealers. He also threatened us with a gun when he found out we suspected him. We somehow escaped and came straight here," Vaishnavi explained.

It looked like the lazy inspector had finally given his full attention upon hearing "drug dealer." Vaishnavi told him our entire story, omitting the parts about my romance, much to my comfort.

"But why did you do all that?" the inspector asked. "You could have come to the police right away."

"Sir, we didn't know it was a criminal case. It was just a mystery to us—where our friend had gone," I explained, regaining my composure.

"Where is Arun's house?" the inspector asked. "We can raid his house to see if there are drugs."

"Sir, we don't know where it is, but the police can find it," I replied.

"Okay, you can go now. We will look into this case. I have registered an F.I.R. against Arun Dutt," the inspector said.

"Sir, I think he may have sent lookout men after us. He even managed to get his hands on the diaries," Vaishnavi added, leaving me amazed at her quick thinking. "I managed to retrieve them during our escape. They can be used as evidence against him since there will be fingerprints on them."

"That's good," the inspector said. "We need to stay in the security of the police station. Arun might not be as unprepared this time."

Vaishnavi added, "Better be armed, sir. He has a rifle."

Inspector Chaudhary got up from his chair.an picked up a rifle . ordering his 3 men to come with us .

<u>19</u>

I, Vaishnavi, Inspector Chaudhary, and three policemen broke into the I.A.H Headquarters. We insisted on coming because we knew the building's layout, including all the entrances and exits, but actually, we didn't trust Mr. Chaudhary to be non-corrupt, so we didn't want to take any chances.

Chaudhary was hesitant, but he had to let us come along. It's tough for policemen in India to decline a request made by a woman. The police could have opened the door, but they decided to break it down to show off.

The police immediately went to Arun's office, where he was still groaning in pain. Arun was soon overpowered by Inspector Chaudhary's men.

"Take his rifle. There will be fingerprints on it, and that will be enough evidence for court," I said.

"Where do you live? Where are the drugs?" Inspector Chaudhary asked as Arun was surrounded by four guns pointed at him.

Arun didn't answer. He just kept panting and cursing. It was a sharp slap from Chaudhary which left a red mark on his cheek.

"Where are the drugs?" Chaudhary asked again, slapping Arun once more.

He remained silent, neither confessing nor claiming his innocence. By then, the entire staff had gathered around to witness the spectacle. Having your boss's boss's boss being slapped by Chaudhary was a sight no one wanted to miss.

Suddenly, Chaudhary's phone buzzed, and one of his men picked it up for him.

"Sir, his home is a minute's ride from our police station, in Ward 4. Looks like he knew he would go to jail, so he bought it to save our petrol," he said. Arun began muttering curses again.

Arun was loaded into the police jeep and taken into custody at the police station. A team of four officers was sent to his house to search for drugs.

We waited for half an hour in the police station while Chaudhary ordered tea for us again. It seemed the inspector functions on tea. I don't drink water as frequently as he drinks tea, but it didn't matter. I was just glad that he was treating a millionaire like any other criminal.

My thoughts drifted back to Vikas. I knew he would be proud. I thanked my stars that our every bet had paid off. There was no question left now.

I still felt guilty for ever suspecting Vaishnavi. She had been my friend for ages, and it made no sense for her to betray me. I wanted to hug her right now.

Soon, Chaudhary's phone buzzed again. The ring startled everyone, as there was very little exchange of words in this meeting.

"Hello, did you find anything at—"

"Yes, sir, we found loads of drugs there, and there were his fingerprints on all of them. We also found a lot of guns. We have enough evidence to put him in jail and prove his guilt in court," Chaudhary smiled, and Arun began shouting curses again. He struggled to free himself from the handcuffs and the grip of Inspector Chaudhary's men, but failed miserably. Soon, he was in Lucknow Central Jail, behind bars.

We got out of there and rode toward our rooms. We were both tired and wanted to sleep for a week, but I was woken up by Vaishnavi after just two hours.

"Bhai, wake up! There are a million things to be done, meeting Jiju for starters," she said.

"Meeting Jiju isn't just the starter; it's the main course," I replied.

"Yay!" she said. "So, we're going to Finland?"

I hugged her.

"Thanks, man. We could have died today."

She laughed again.
"All adds to the fun of it."

"What?"

"It would make a great novel. I'm writing it."

"You are not allowed to share our romance with the public."

"I'll just change the names. The girl's name will be Vikas, and the boy's name will be Akansha."

"That was a horrible joke."

"All adds to the fun of it."

"You know, by the way you were acting, I thought you were mixed up with Arun."

"Not every friend betrays. Get betrayal out of your subconscious."

I smiled, and out of nowhere, I jumped in the air.

"Stop jumping. Book tickets to Helsinki."

"What's that?"

"Where Jiju is! You didn't even Google the capital of Finland?"

"Let's go, then."

We still had no clue where in Helsinki we would find Vikas, but okay, we had reached this far. We'd clear the last stage and meet Vikas. I did a little dance when I realized I was about to see him after so long. I couldn't help but smile, especially since we had both confessed our feelings. Vaishnavi had a naughty smile on her face.

"Stop smiling like that. It's getting on my nerves."

"Stop smiling like what? I just like the view," she said, sounding very innocent for Vaishnavi.

"Huh, you are seriously an awful human being."

"Hey?" she said in the same tone.

"Were you born crazy, or did you become like that after being hit by a leather ball on your head?"

"You're the one who likes playing cricket, and you're the one who likes watching it with Jiju."

"You're seriously an awful human being."

"Will you say that every time I say Jiju?" she asked, grinning from ear to ear.

"Seriously awful."

"I may be, but Jiju is not."

"Stop it," I said, as my cheeks turned the color of tomatoes.

"Did you do a course on craziness?" I asked.

"You don't need courses for everything. Did you do a course to fall in love with Jiju?"

The flight was peaceful, except for Vaishnavi's occasional "Jiju" chant.

"How are we going to find your Jiju, by the way?" I asked, munching on aeroplane fries.

"We'll ask people if an Indian has come to live here recently."

"If someone from Finland came to Ahmedabad, would we have known?" I asked.

"We'll find him in a day or two if he doesn't find us. He might even be holding a garland for us," Vaishnavi said, taking a sip of her paper boat juice.

"Want to ask the airport staff if an Indian came here recently?" I asked.

"Is the manager your uncle, that they will tell you? She'll find him. Don't worry," she said, tapping my shoulder.

"Glad you didn't say, 'We will find Jiju.'" I said, and we both burst into laughter.

We landed in Finland in the afternoon, and the bright sun glowed pleasantly over our heads. Helsinki, the capital city of the happiest country in the world, was glowing at its best. It was a pleasure to know that Finland's education system didn't pressurize students, making it one of the best in the world. People like me and Vikas would fall in love with this place, where happiness thrives. I felt happy that Vikas chose this place for his escape. It's easy to guess why someone who owns a mental health company, dedicated to making India happy, would choose Finland.

My heart did its disco dance again. I was about to see him. I could say it with certainty now—there was no longer any doubt in my walnut-shaped brain and my excited heart. We decided to settle into a traditional Finnish restaurant as we were starving, and the mouthwatering food was irresistible. We were surprised to find tea there— Indian chai, to be specific.

We couldn't help but ask the waiter, "How did you get Indian tea on your menu?"

The waiter responded, "It wasn't on the menu before, but a gentleman from India came a week ago, asked us to try Indian tea, and recommended we offer it to other customers. The chef liked it, so we added it to the menu. We also have pakoras now."

I almost jumped out of my seat. "When does the man come to your restaurant?" I asked eagerly, sipping my tea, knowing it was there because of Vikas.

"He comes in the evening, around 4 pm."

I smiled at Vaishnavi and turned toward the waiter. "Bring some pakoras too. I'm starving."

The waiter got a big tip that day.

After exploring Helsinki's beautiful capital, we returned to the restaurant around 3:30 pm. We ordered lunch and, while eating Finnish pastries filled with rice porridge, we waited for him. It's funny how we didn't even have to search for him in Helsinki. As the clock ticked by, my excitement grew. We finished our Finnish food, but it was still 3:50, and he hadn't arrived yet. So, we ordered some butter milk and sipped the Finnish-style Lassi gratefully.

And then he came.

We hid our butter milk-stained faces. We wanted to surprise him and didn't want him to notice us too soon. But I couldn't help but notice every little detail about him—his hazel brown eyes, his chocolate brown hair, the way he sipped his tea, the way he ordered, and the way he left the restaurant after finishing his pastries and tea.

"What are you looking at? Let's follow him. Don't you want to surprise Jiju?" Vaishnavi said, winking.

We tiptoed behind him through the streets of Helsinki. My heart was thumping faster than the aeroplane we'd flown in. We were just inches away from him.

"Go hug him from behind. I want to see his face when he realizes it's you, and I want to see your face when you meet Jiju," Vaishnavi said with a grin.

I couldn't stop grinning. Without saying a word, without making a sound, I hugged him from behind. Time stood still, like we were back in the fields of Saint Stephen's. His first reaction was panic, but as soon as he realized who was holding him so tightly, his expression changed. He hugged me back. There was so much to say, so much to discuss, but at that moment, nothing mattered except him and me. The rest of the world disappeared, and we just tightly hugged each other. My eyes met his, and we realized that both of our eyes were wet. My heart felt normal again.my heart was not doing a disco dance. There's something magical about being in the arms of a loved one that just comforts you.

The three of us walked toward nowhere. Then, Vikas asked the second most important question hovering in his mind:

"Did you read my diaries?"

"Yes, Vikas. Arun is in jail,"

"I love you, Vikas," I said, not waiting for him to ask the most important question.

We were soon back on the airplane that would take us back to India. Vikas didn't want to stay in Lucknow, so he planned to buy or rent a house or an apartment in Ahmedabad. I planned to submit my paper at Rani Lakshmi Bai college and file for resignation. Vaishnavi has begun typing her novel about us and is naming it The Background Music. I spent hours discussing my business with him.s As the plane took off, I rested my head on his shoulder and relaxed like I hadn't in a long time. The best part about crazy things is how comfortably you can sleep when they're happening.